PANTHER CITY

TALES OF A GEN X GRADE 3 CLASS PROJECT RUN AMOK

AYUN HALLIDAY

ILLUSTRATIONS BY LENI YOW-FAIRS

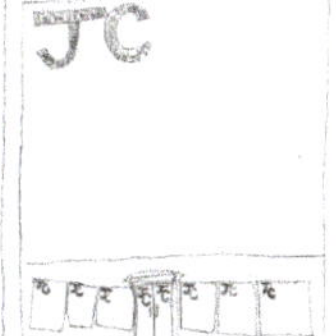

Cover art and book design by Ayun Halliday

www.AyunHalliday.com

Published by Theater of the Apes
an imprint of Literary Kitchen
www.theater-of-the-apes.com/library/
First edition

ISBN: 978-1-950272-47-1

JANUARY

We are making a city. It'll cover all three bulletin boards when we're done. We have to bring stuff in from home to make it with.

"What kind of stuff?" Steven S asked.

"Paper stuff," Mrs. Voss said. "Magazines. Old greeting cards."

Stacy N stuck her hand up. She's always sticking her hand up. "What about cereal boxes?" she said. Mrs. Voss said okay, and Stacy looked around like she'd had some great idea nobody'd ever thought of before.

She thinks she's big coz last fall, when we were in 2nd grade, the class who brought in the most Box Tops for Education got a pizza party and she brought in the most. Big whoop. Everybody knows she bribed her brothers to give her their box tops. She's got about a million of them. They said okay, so long as she gave them the prize from the bottom of the box every time it was her turn to keep it. That's cheating.

I'm glad I don't have any brothers OR sisters! I don't have to share my room and I get lots and lots of Christmas presents.

The only thing I wish is that Mom would buy the kinds of cereal Stacy N's mom buys. She won't buy me Count Chocula or Lucky Charms or Kaboom or ANYTHING with unnecessary sugar. Boo!

She bought me a couple of boxes of Cheez-Its coz they have Box Tops for Education, too. It's not just cereals. "See?" she said. "You don't have to eat a bunch of junky-junk to participate."

I wish crackers came with prizes inside the box.

After we brought in all our paper stuff from home, Mrs. Voss said it was time to get started. The first thing was to brainstorm the different types of places a city has.

Lee Lindstrom raised her hand. "Pet shop," she said.

Stacy N raised her hand and said, "Church."

Steven E raised his and said, "Temple."

Temple's where him and Stacy Zimmerman go instead of church. It's on the way to ballet class. It's a lot newer looking than church. It's very mod. No steeple or stained glass windows or anything.

"Keep going," Mrs. Voss said.

"Doctor's office," said Stacy Z, coz that's where her dad works. She says he's famous coz he separated a pair of Siamese twins. They were joined at the HEAD! A bunch of other people's dads are doctors, too. Samantha's MOM is a doctor. A sex doctor.

"What else?" said Mrs. Voss.

The boys raised their hands. "Gas station," they said. "Fire station. Police station."

"Very good," Mrs. Voss said. She waited to see if anyone could think of any other city places. We couldn't, so she said, "What about a grocery store? Or a TV station?"

Oh yeah! My grandfather worked in a radio station before he retired! They let him bring home a bunch of 8-track tapes nobody wanted! Van Cliburn and Percy Faith and <u>Fiddler on the Roof</u>. He was an engineer. Not the train kind.

People got really excited and started shouting out ideas coz they didn't want anyone else to think of them first. "Burger Chef! Dry cleaner! School! Bank!"

"Wow!" Mrs. Voss told us. "I'm glad your wheels are turning so quickly, but let's not forget to raise our hands."

I stuck mine up as high as it can go and waved it around, even though we're not supposed to.

Mrs. Voss called on me anyway. She was laughing a little when she said my name, probably coz she's not used to seeing me acting like I've got ants in my pants.

"Can I make the newspaper?" I said.

"A newspaper's not a building, dummy," Kevin Dupree whispered. He sits right behind me. That's how come I could hear him. I wish Mrs. Voss had heard him, too.

Then he'd be in trouble without anyone calling me a tattlepants.

A newspaper is so a building! It's red brick and my mom works in the Women's section. She writes about all sorts of stuff. Fancy parties and how people decorate their houses and this family that had a pet deer.

Sometimes when there's no school, Mom takes me to the Women's section with her. There's a bunch of steno pads and soft black pencils and I can have as many as I want to make drawings with.

When I get sick of doing that, she pays me a quarter to stuff the brides' pictures back inside their self addressed stamped envelopes. That's how they get them back after they're published in the Weddings and Engagements column.

Before that though, the guys in the Sports section pick one to be the winner of their Dog of the Week contest.

The brides don't know about the contest. Mom says I'm not allowed to tell. It would hurt their feelings if they knew.

I messed up! I wrote Indianapolis Star on top of our city's newspaper. I forgot we were supposed to use made up names! Mrs. Voss said it's not worth getting so upset over. I can fix it with a little piece of paper and some tape after we decide what to name our city, like how the first settlers came up with Jamestown.

Everybody had to think one up and then we would vote to see which name would be the winner.

Lee Lindstrom raised her hand. "If we do it that way, everyone will just vote for their own and nothing will win," she said.

Mrs. Voss smiled like she couldn't believe the smartness of Lee. "How about this?" She said. "Instead of one vote, everybody gets two votes?"

Lee raised her hand again. "And you can't vote for the same name twice," she said.

"Right," Mrs. Voss said. "You have to pick two."

Lee raised her hand again, but Mrs. Voss said she didn't want to turn this into a big, fat, hairy deal, that three rules was good enough. One, everybody has to suggest one name. Two, everybody gets two votes. Three, you can only vote for your own once. She picked up a piece of chalk so she could write our suggestions on the blackboard.

"Princetown," said Steven S.

"Rexland," said Jamie Craig.

"Mittensville," said Stacy Z.

"Wait a minute," Mrs. Voss said. "Are those your pets' names?" She started erasing the board. "You need to pick something that will be meaningful to everyone, not just yourself."

She gave us another minute to think, then we said our suggestions and she wrote them on the board and then we voted.

The winner was Chocolate City. Except when we got back from lunch, Mrs. Voss told us that Principal Moncrieff told her we had to come up with a different name. She wouldn't say why.

Lee Lindstrom bet it's coz of slow readers not knowing how to spell hard words like chocolate.

I bet it's coz chocolate has a lot of sugar and sugar's not good for you.

Kimberly said it's coz of Chocolate City being a real place. She says Chocolate City's another name for Washington DC. It means there's a lot of Black people there.

"That's prejudiced!" Ginny Schmidt said. She thinks she's so tuff, but ha ha on you, Ginny. Kimberly can't be prejudiced. She's Black! She's the only Black kid in 3rd grade and her brother and sister are the only Black kids in first grade. They're twins.

No offense to Kimberly, but I think she's wrong about Chocolate City. I don't think anybody calls Washington DC that. My grandparents were there last year. They sent me a postcard of the White House and then they went to Colonial Williamsburg and bought me a tricorn hat and a plastic sculpture of Abe Lincoln sitting in a chair. If there were a lot of Black people, I think they would've said.

Steven S said Hershey, Pennsylvania's a real Chocolate City. They've got an amusement park there that's MADE out of chocolate.

Mrs. Voss put her hand up. We know what that means. Mouths shut. No one can say a single word til we've showed her we know how to pay attention. After about a million years, she said, okay, and had us tell her our suggestions all over again coz she'd erased them all while we were at lunch.

"Do we still vote twice?" Stacy N asked.

"Can we vote for a different one if we want?" Stacy Z asked.

"If we thought up a better suggestion than the one we said before, can we say that instead?" Kimberly asked.

Mrs. Voss took a deep breath and closed her eyes. She does that whenever she feels like yelling. "Did you think of a better one, Kimberly?" she asked. Kimberly nodded. "Okay, what is it?"

"Panther City," Kimberly said.

Mrs. Voss raised her eyebrows all the way up to the top of her head. "Because of our school mascot?" she asked after a second. Kimberly nodded. "Brilliant," Mrs. Voss said and picked up the chalk. We voted again and this time, Kimberly's suggestion won.

If you get done with your worksheet before everybody else, you can decide between quiet reading or going to Panther City HQ.

Panther City HQ is a long table Mrs. Voss got the maintenance man, Mr. Jenks, to set up for us. It's got all our construction paper and the paper stuff we brought in from home and scissors and glue sticks. It's okay to leave it set up, as long as we keep things tidy and not make more work for Mr. Jenks when he comes in after school to vacuum and empty the trash.

Quiet reading used to be my favorite, but now it's Panther City!

After the newspaper, I made a house coz a city has to have a whole big bunch of those. Anybody who wants to can make one. I wish people would make them their own way, instead of copying me. All the girls want to make them the same as me coz of how good I am at bricks.

First you make a bunch of long lines, then you go back and put the up and down lines in. If you do it wrong, it looks like checks, not bricks.

Stacy N and Stacy Z and Ginny's bricks look so babyish, it's embarrassing. I don't think Mrs. Voss should've let them hang their houses up next to mine. She should've made them do them over out of wood or stones or something.

Mrs. Voss called me up to her desk for a private conversation. She said she knows how important Panther City is to me, but this is a group project so that requires a bit of cooperation. "You know what that means, right?"

Is she kidding? Even a nursery schooler knows that word.

"It means sometimes we have to accept that things will turn out a little differently than they would if we were doing them by ourselves."

I said, "I know, but they're using up all the red construction paper and they don't even know how to do bricks!"

She tapped her finger on the spot between my eyebrows. My worry spot, she calls it. "Guess what," she said. "There's a whole 'nother pack of red construction paper in the supply closet."

I love my teacher but I'm still worried.

Ginny copied again! Making a swimming pool was MY idea! Mine is the same as the one where Heather's mom's boyfriend lives. Heather's mom took us over there one time and me and Heather were the only ones in the whole pool. There were a bunch of adults, but they just sat around getting suntans. His apartment had air conditioning and wall to wall shag carpet and a built-in bar. I'm gonna live in a condo complex when I grow up.

I don't know how to make a condo complex so I made more houses and put the pool up next to them and called it a condo complex.

Ginny says her pool's better than mine coz it's at a country club. She's gonna make a bunch of other stuff to go with it. A golf course and a parking lot and a main building, and a patio with umbrella tables where people can order hamburgers while their kids swim. You have to be a member though.

Know what Kimberly told me? You can't go to Ginny's country club if you're Black. Not the one in Panther City. The one her family goes to in real life.

"What if Ginny has her birthday party there and every girl in class is invited?" I said.

"Nope," Kimberly said.

That is so mean! I felt so bad for Kimberly but she said don't. Her cousins live a block away from her and they have a Penguin pool she can swim in any time she feels like. Not now. In summer, when it's warm enough. Lucky.

Kimberly is making a lawyer's office.

"Good idea," said Mrs. Voss.

We took a field trip to the Indiana Statehouse. It was kind of boring except for the ceiling which is a dome made out of stained glass. The part of the building it's in is called a rotunda.

"Rotunda means fat butt!" Steven S shouted.

Mrs. Voss made him be partners with her for the rest of the trip.

When we got back to school, Mrs. Voss asked for volunteers to make a Panther City Statehouse.

Nobody raised their hand except Lee Lindstrom. Everybody else thinks government is boring. Lee gets As in everything. Math. Reading. Sports. History. She's also the prettiest and most popular.

Mrs. Voss acted disappointed that Lee was the only one who wanted to make Panther City a Statehouse. "I think it sounds like a really fun challenge!" she said. "Remember the big dome in the rotunda!"

Steven S made a farting noise and we all got in trouble.

Lee Lindstrom

Everybody wants to make a toy store. Mrs. Voss said she gets it but the point of Panther City isn't for everyone to do the same thing. It's to make a city with lots of different kinds of businesses, just like in real life, and 15 toy stores are too many. Maybe if its population was in the millions like New York City or something, you could have that many, but Panther City isn't that big. "So how can we settle this fairly?" she asked.

We told her we could vote.

"Okay," she said. "What are we voting on?"

"Who gets to do the toy store," we said.

"No," she told us. "What's the criteria? Our metric for deciding?"

Huh?

"How do you determine who you're going to vote for?" she said.

Stacy N raised her hand. "You could put everyone's names on the board and we could vote for anyone we want except ourself."

"Hmm," Mrs. Voss said. "That's what we call a popularity contest. The problem with that is the same people tend to win over and over." Everyone looked at Lee Lindstrom, including Mrs. Voss.

I raised my hand. "What if everybody who wants to make a toy store makes a toy store and the best one's the one we put on the board?"

Mrs. Voss nodded like she liked that answer better. "Meritocracy," she said. "Does anyone know what that word means?"

"Being the best artist?" I said.

"It could mean that, I guess," she said. "A meritocracy is a system that awards excellence. But we also want to make sure we're using our time wisely. It'd be a shame for people to waste a lot of class time making things they won't get to put up."

Me and Lee and Jasper said we didn't mind.

"Nice try," Mrs. Voss said, like of course the best artists in class would say they didn't mind. I'm not being conceited. Everybody knows.

"Tell you what," Mrs. Voss said. "Let's put everybody's name in a hat and whoever's name gets picked gets to draw the toy store."

We didn't have a hat so we took the Kleenex out of the class Kleenex box and used that. Mrs. Voss thought of a number and the person who got closest to that number got to pick the name out of the box. Jasper said 23 and she was thinking of 24, so he got to pick. She held the box over his head, so he couldn't peek, even though he wouldn't have.

Guess whose name he picked.

Lee Lindstrom

Lee Lindstrom

Panther City's got two movie theaters. A regular one and a drive-in. Steven E made both.

It's kind of hard to tell what the drive-in is. Just a big rectangle up on these ladder things. It's supposed to be the screen. He wanted to make a lot of cars to go with it but Mrs. Voss told him, "No way, José." If she let one boy draw a bunch of cars, there'd be no end. Every boy in class would be drawing cars and nothing else.

Steven E should make a playground in front of the drive-in screen to play in before the movie starts. It's pretty fun, even though the equipment's the old-fashioned, dangerous kind. The only thing I don't like is my mom makes me wear pajamas to the drive-in. She wants me to be all ready when it's time to lie down in the backseat and go to sleep. All the other kids on the playground get to wear their regular clothes.

We haven't been to the drive-in in a long time, though. Next time I see Daddy, I'm gonna ask him to take me there next summer. He won't make me wear pajamas. He'll let me sit up front with him and watch the whole movie. I hate having to lie down in back.

This one time, the movie was <u>Anne of a Thousand Days</u>. I kept peeking up over the top of the seat coz I wanted to see the part where Anne Boleyn gets her head chopped off. But then I fell asleep and missed it.

Jasper is making the hospital. It's bigger than the biggest building in Panther City. It's the size of a whole entire sheet of paper. It looks kind of weird, but Mrs. Voss said you want a hospital to be big coz they're like mini cities inside.

Then she had us say the names of all the different people who work in a hospital.

Doctors. Duh.

Nurses. Duh.

Ambulance guys.

"Secretaries," said Stacy Z.

Steven S stuck his hand up and when Mrs. Voss called on him, he said, "Maintenance men for mopping up all the blood and pee!"

We all got in trouble for laughing and had to put our heads down on our desks for a whole minute. Steven got in extra trouble for saying pee.

"What are some other types of jobs people might have in a hospital?" Mrs. Voss asked, when we were allowed to lift our heads back up. "Jasper?"

"Parking lot attendant," Jasper said. "The ladies in the gift shop. The people who work in the cafeteria. Security guards. Chaplain. The teenage girls who push the carts with candy and magazines and crosswords and stuff. The other patients and their families."

Boy! Jasper sure knows a lot about hospitals!

FEBRUARY

We got in trouble coz somebody drew some boobs on Panther City's Drive-In.

Mrs. Voss didn't even notice til Steven S and all the boys started laughing and saying the boobs belonged to Linda Lovelace.

Linda Lovelace's movies are all XXX.

Mrs. Voss took the drive-in off the bulletin board and put it in her purse. She asked us did we want her to leave a note for Mr. Jenks, telling him to take the whole thing down when he came that night.

What? NO! A couple of girls started crying. I didn't, but I felt like it.

"Enough drama, girls," Mrs. Voss said. "Everyone take out Adventures in Science. Turn to where we left off. Page 33, I think."

WHO CARES ABOUT STUPID PLANT SYSTEMS???

Right before the bell rang, Mrs. Voss told us she'd decided to give us another chance to show her we're mature enough to handle the responsibility of Panther City. That Panther City is a privilege, not a right. "I'd advise you to keep that in mind if you're considering behaving in a way other than proper ladies and gentlemen," she said. "Do we understand each other?"

Everyone nodded and said, "Yes, Mrs. Voss."

We waited til we were at our cubbies getting our backpacks, then me and Heather and Stacy Z started jumping around in a circle hugging each other, we were so happy. We wanted to scream but we had to do it with no sound coming out coz Mrs. Voss was still in a bad mood.

If I had come in the next day, and Panther City wasn't up on the bulletin boards, I would've had a CONNIPTION! I would have found out who drew those boobs and called his parents to make them pull down his pants and give him a spanking in front of the whole school.

Our special guest in class today was Mrs. Voss's husband, Richard. He kept calling her "Annie." Nobody calls teachers by their first names. Just Miss and Mrs. or Mr. if the teacher is a boy, or a maintenance man or something. It made me feel weird. People kept turning around in their seats and looking at me, coz they thought it was funny, Mrs. Voss's husband calling her the same name as my name.

He told us his job is architect. Steven S raised his hand and said, "We know!" coz Mrs. Voss told us ahead of time. Mrs. Voss gave Steven a look like careful, Buster, but her husband just laughed.

Architect's not the same thing as guys in hard hats. He told us their jobs are important too, coz they're the ones who build the buildings, but his job comes before. You have to know how to use a ruler and keep checking your work and be detail oriented, but there's lots of room for creativity, too. He told us it's like being an artist, except you can actually earn a decent living.

"Do any of you guys want to be an artist when you grow up?" he said.

I raised my hand. So did Jasper.

He asked Jasper what he liked to draw. Jasper said tanks, planes and monsters.

"Right on!" Mrs. Voss's husband Richard held his hand up like he was waiting for Jasper to slap him five even though there was no way Jasper could reach that far. His desk is in the third row. Mrs. Voss's husband told Jasper he should definitely consider studying architecture after he graduates from high school.

"What about you?" he asked me. "What do you like to draw?"
I told him I like to draw weddings where everyone's a cat.

"Oh my god, that's the cutest thing I've ever heard!" he said.
"What's your name, sweetie?"

"Annie," I said.

He looked over at Mrs. Voss like for real? She nodded and winked
at me like it was a trick we thought up.

"Well, listen, Annie," he told me, "You've got plenty of time to
figure things out. Maybe you can grow up to be a teacher like
Mrs. Voss."

Stacy N made a ballet school. She goes to a different one than me. I asked her do they get to wear tutus at hers and she said yes. What a rip!

When my mom was signing me up for ballet, she asked the teacher where to go to buy my shoes and stuff. The teacher gave her the name of a store across the street from the mall that sells regular kid's clothes. She said to tell the saleslady that I was one of hers, and that we wanted the beginner package.

So my mom told the saleslady all of that and the saleslady gave her a pair of black shoes and a bag with some pale pink tights and a short sleeved black leotard. No tutu!

We don't even get tutus for recitals.

Stacy told me she got two costumes for her last recital, one for ballet and one for tap, coz her ballet school teaches all different kinds of dancing. For ballet, her costume was a yellow tutu, and for tap, it was a feather boa, gloves and a red sequin one piece with a matching Charlie Chaplin hat. Lucky!

I wish I'd thought of making a ballet school before Stacy coz Mrs. Voss is getting really sick of everybody wanting to make the same things as everybody else. So, instead, I asked could I make a tutu shop to put next door to Stacy's ballet school and she said, "If that's what floats your boat."

Good thing she doesn't have kids yet. If she did, and one of those kids was a girl, she'd know there's no such thing as a tutu shop. Just dance schools that give you costumes with sequins and feathers and dance schools that send your mom to a regular old store to buy the beginner package.

I like it when shops spell "shop" the fancy way.

Everybody hates Jamie Craig coz he's a such a whiny little liar baby. He keeps making department stores and writing J.C. across the top.

He told Steven S and Steven E and Ginny and a bunch of other people who wanted to beat him up that it stands for JCPenney, but that's a lie. Number one, you're not supposed to have the names of real things in Panther City, and number two, you're not allowed to name things after yourself or your pets.

Panther City must belong to everybody equally!

Steven S's big brother says what are we, a bunch of 3rd grade commies?

Steven S's brother is in high school. He can drive a car. It's coz of him Steven knows so much about sex and commies and hippies and other stuff kids our age aren't supposed to know about.

Steven's making up a funny story about people who eat magical cookies that make their boobs and dicks grow really big. He makes up a little more every day and tells it to us at recess, back behind the swings where there's a bush we like to hide behind.

If Mrs. Voss found out we'd be in so much trouble!

oday we talked about monuments. Monuments are
sculptures that you stick around a city. They are mostly of
dead people, but they can also be just shapes, like the one
downtown on the Circle. It's kind of like the Eiffel Tower with a
big skinny part sticking up. At Christmas, they string lights down
from the top of it so it looks like a Christmas tree, but not really.

I thought the monument was just so people'd know what city they
were in, like Paris, but Mrs. Voss said no, that every monument is
erected to honor a person or event, even if it doesn't look like it.

Steven S said, "Erected!" and then him and some of the boys
laughed. I don't get it.

Mrs. Voss pretended she didn't hear.

"Next time you're downtown, ask your parents to stop the car on
the Circle and show you where the plaque is on the monument.
All the names on it are the names of Indianapolis boys who gave
their lives defending our country in a war."

Kimberly raised her hand and said, "Not Vietnam."

Mrs. Voss nodded like she thought that was right, but she didn't
know for sure. Kimberly said her mother's cousin went to Vietnam
and got shot dead right away. Mrs. Voss said she was very sorry to
hear that but that we should probably stay on topic.

The only dead person I know is my great-grandmother Dooley.
She's not my real great-grandmother. I just called her that.
Grampy's real mom ran away when he was just a little baby, and
then later after he was all grown up, his dad married Dooley and
took her on a big honeymoon all over Europe. Sometimes when
Grampy is being funny he'll rub his eyes like he's crying and say,

"Wahh! Wahh! I miss my mommy." He's so silly.

Mrs. Voss had us make a list of people for our Panther City monuments.

Stacy N asked if it was okay to say alive people, or did they all have to be dead, like Kimberly's mom's cousin.

"Ooh, Stacy's afraid of ghosts," Steven S said.

"Shut up!" Stacy said. "Am not!"

"I think we can have some living people," Mrs. Voss said. "Provided they've achieved something of note. Also, let's refrain from telling our classmates to shut up."

"Can we make a monument of you?" I asked.

"Brown nose!" Kevin Dupree whispered. I'm not even gonna say what that means, it's so rude.

"I'm flattered, but no," Mrs. Voss said. "Who are your heroes?"

Mrs. Voss IS my hero.

We made a list and voted and the winners were George Washington, Joe Namath, Muhammad Ali and Cowboy Bob. The only one I voted for was Cowboy Bob. He does the cartoons at lunchtime on Channel 4. He has brown hair and brown eyes and a dog named Tumbleweed and a puppet named Sourdough the Singing Biscuit who sings so bad, Cowboy Bob rolls his eyes and says, "I think it's time for another cartoon!" One of the best things about vacation is eating lunch on a tray in front of Cowboy Bob.

Lee Lindstrom asked could Panther City have some women monuments too, because of Women's Lib.

"Good idea," said Mrs. Voss. So we said some more names and

voted and this time the winners were Olga Korbut and Billie Jean King.

Olga Korbut is that gymnast girl from Russia who had never tasted catsup before she got here. Now she eats it all the time. She loves it so much, she eats a bowl of it for breakfast! Yuck!

Billie Jean King is the tennis lady who whooped Bobby Riggs' male chauvinist pig butt! Yay! Girl power!

Mrs. Voss said maybe it would be good to expand beyond the wide, wide world of sports, so we picked Betsy Ross, too, and I get to do her.

My mom got very excited when she heard I was doing Betsy Ross. She said I should talk to Gran and Grampy coz of them having gone to Colonial Williamsburg on their trip to Washington DC. They saw people do stuff like candlemaking and soapmaking and showing visitors how mattresses were stuffed with straw or feathers, and how if you woke up in the middle of the night and needed to pee, instead of a toilet, you had to use a chamber pot under your bed.

My mom has a chamber pot, but she just uses it to store potpourri in. It's an antique. She thinks antiques are neat coz they're so old. Not me! I like mod stuff like Dawn dolls and the Honeycomb Kids! Don't trust anyone over the age of 30!

Gran says the people who work in Colonial Williamsburg have to dress up like it's two hundred years ago, the way they do on Connor Prairie Farm, which is the oldest place in Indianapolis. We took a field trip there in second grade. They showed us how to carry muskets and make corn husk dolls. The blacksmith was wearing tube socks. Everyone bought old-fashioned stick candy in the gift shop. My friends all picked watermelon. I picked sarsaparilla coz of the Bugs Bunny cartoon where Yosemite Sam says, "Gimme a sarsaparilla and make it snappy!" It tasted like root beer.

Grampy says Panther City sounds like a lot of fun but Betsy Ross lived in Philadelphia, not Colonial Williamsburg.

I found out the saddest thing. The reason Jasper made the hospital is his little sister's really sick and she's gonna die. She's got the same disease as the one in <u>Brian's Song</u>, which is the saddest movie ever. I didn't see it but Lee Lindstrom did and she told us the whole story of it. She made her parents buy her the record of it.

The saddest movie I ever saw was <u>Born Free</u>. The people in it had had Elsa the Lioness since she was an orphaned cub, but in the end, they can't keep her anymore. They have to let her go off to live with the other lions coz she was born free.

It was on TV when I was little and my parents let me pick: I could either go to bed at the next commercial or go to bed at 8 o'clock. I picked the next commercial.

The next commercial came on like 2 seconds later. NO FAIR!

Last year, it came on TV again, and Mom let me stay up for the whole thing.

I hope I get to see the whole thing of <u>Brian's Song</u> some day.

I feel so bad for Jasper. I didn't even know he had a sister.

Not to brag but my monument of Betsy Ross beats all the other monuments' butts.

I'm the only one in class who knows how to draw mouths and eyes.

Ginny's origami paper got us girls in trouble. No fair! I didn't do ANYTHING!

The paper was little squares with flowers or birds or designs made out of real gold on the front. The backs were just plain white though.

Ginny wanted to be the boss of who got to use it coz she was the one who brought it in, and it's really expensive.

She let me and Stacy Z and Lee Lindstrom and some of the others use some but not Samantha, coz when she spent the night at Samantha's, Samantha's mom the sex doctor wouldn't let her be excused from the table until she ate half of everything on her plate, even though she told her she was allergic!

Plus, she says their house smells bad and they have this mean old poodle with runny eyes named Lovebug who wears a diaper.

I'm glad I've never gotten invited to spend the night there!

Samantha started crying coz of it being only her and the boys not being allowed to take any origami paper. "Shut up, crybaby!" Ginny said, and pinched her.

When Mrs. Voss looked up from her desk to ask what was going on back there, Samantha tattled.

So Mrs. Voss took all the origami paper away from Panther City HQ and put it in her drawer, because she expected better of us. That's what she said. That Panther City is a community and community means finding ways to work together and share resources with everyone in the community.

Ginny said yes but that the origami paper was really special coz she got it in her Christmas stocking and it came all the way from Japan and the reason she didn't want to share it is some of the people in the community were trying to hog it all for themselves instead of just using a little bit.

Ginny's father is a lawyer.

I don't think Samantha was trying to hog origami paper.

Her nose kind of looks like a pig nose though.

MARCH

Ginny had her birthday at Farrell's and all the girls in class were invited, even Samantha.

Farrell's is the new restaurant at Castleton Mall. It's got an old-fashioned theme and the greatest menu ever! It's all sundaes and stuff! They've got regular food, too, but nobody orders that.

If it's your birthday, there's this giant sundae you can order called a Zoo. It's this enormous silver bowl filled with whipped cream and cherries and nuts and chocolate sauce and all different kinds of ice cream flavors all mixed together.

The reason it's called a Zoo is there's all these little plastic animals on top of it. All of us got one to keep. Ginny got the biggest, coz she was the birthday girl. It was a giraffe with a really long neck. I got a monkey. There were lots of monkeys but only one giraffe.

Whenever anybody get a Zoo, a siren goes off and one of the waiters runs over to thump a big drum like the kind from a parade, then two more waiters run all over the restaurant, carrying the Zoo on a stretcher, pretending like they don't know which table they're supposed to take it to! It was so funny! After they put it down, all the other waiters and waitresses came over and made Ginny stand on a chair, wearing an old-fashioned styrofoam hat, while we sang Happy Birthday to her.

There were two other kids who got Zoos while we were there. We sang Happy Birthday to them, too, even though we didn't know them.

I'm going to ask my mom if I can have my next birthday there.

On the way out, there's all these old-fashioned jars filled with old-

fashioned candy. It's for sale. Mrs. Schmidt said we could each pick
one thing to be our party favor. A bunch of people picked these
long strips of paper with colored candy dots stuck to them. I picked
Gold Mine gum. It comes in a cloth bag with Old West style
writing on it that you can put stuff in after you've eaten up all
the gum.

They had sarsaparilla sticks like I got at Connor Prairie Farm, but I
wanted something big.

When I grow up, I am DEFINITELY working at Farrell's.

Ginny said no fair that I made Farrell's for Panther City when
she's the one who had her birthday there.

Big whoop! Lee is having her birthday there next month and so are
both of the Stacys.

Also, Mrs. Voss doesn't let us use real life place names for Panther
City, so it's not even Farrell's.

It's Gold Mine Old Timey Candy Shoppe & Ice Cream Parlor.

The "and" symbol makes things look extra old-fashioned. I'm the
only one in class who knows how to make one.

GOLD MINE
OLD TIMEY
CANDY SHOPPE
&
ICE-CREAM PARLOR

One day Mrs. Voss said, "Who here thinks Panther City needs a zoo?"

(A real one, not the Farrell's kind. Haha. It's coz we're doing animal habitats in science.)

Everyone started waving their hands and going "ooh ooh ooh," trying to get her to pick them, but I kept mine in my lap coz she never picks the people who go "ooh ooh ooh."

But then she didn't pick anybody. We have to do it in groups and Mrs. Voss already decided who's in which group.

Mine is Lee Lindstrom, Steven S and Jamie C (barf).

Each group had to elect someone from their group to pick the name of their animal out of a hat.

We elected Lee and she picked elephant. Boo. I wanted lion or monkey. Oh well. At least we didn't get snake like Ginny and Heather and Kimberly and Steven E. Ginny cried.

Mrs. Voss said, "Remember, you're designing habitats. It's not about drawing animals." She told us to think about what elements we could put in our habitats to make our animals feel less homesick. Like if it's a monkey, you could put in some branches and bananas and stuff.

Lee said we should make a mommy elephant and a baby elephant and that the baby should hold onto the mommy's tail with its trunk the way they do on Mutual of Omaha's Wild Kingdom.

Lee made the mommy and I made the baby.

Steven S cut out a bunch of brown Hershey's Kiss-looking things to be their poo!

Jamie was supposed to be making the cement part for them to walk around on, but he kept stopping to make more department stores.

Spring Vacation starts Friday and I'm so sad. No Panther City for nine whole days!

Some of us asked Mrs. Voss if we could keep working on it while we're on vacation, but she said no, that we should all take a little break to just enjoy our vacations.

I would enjoy my vacation a lot more if I could work on Panther City.

A lot of kids are going to Florida.

Lee Lindstrom's parents are taking her and her brother Mark to St. Martin so they can practice their French. It is an island with palm trees and beaches and a lot of Black people. Lee said she wishes she could take Kimberly with her but the plane tickets were really expensive, so she's not allowed to bring guests. Kimberly told me she's glad. She'd rather go to Chicago to see her cousins.

I'm not going anywhere. Mom says a week is too long for her to be bringing me in to the newspaper with her, so I have to go to Gran and Grampy's for all but one day of it. Boo! I miss my friends and there's nothing to do! At least I get to watch Cowboy Bob. Before him is Gran's favorite, <u>The Bob Braun Show</u>. It's so boring. It's worse than <u>Merv Griffin</u>! The only thing I like is when Bob and the two blonde ladies do commercials for their favorite products. They're not real commercials. They just hold things up and tell you why they're such great products. They're never for stuff you've heard of, like in a real commercial. The best ones are for Ava Gabor wigs. Bob says they look so glamorous, he wishes he could wear one, too! I don't think they look very glamorous at all. I like long hair. The only person I know who wears a wig is my other grandma, Teensy. She lives in Arizona.

APRIL

How I spent my Spring vacation

By Annie

I got up and ate breakfast and watched cartoons and then I went to my grandparents'. My grandfather smokes a pipe. He is retired. My grandmother likes watching Bob Braun and making cookies. She wants me to be her assistant and help her cook and clean and wash clothes. Her washing machine is an antique. It has a thing called a mangle. You have to be very careful because if your hand gets caught in it, it could tear your arm off.

One day they took me to Farrell's for lunch. A man at the table next to us got a thing called The Trough. It is potatoes and hamburger meat and stuff, not ice cream. If you eat the whole thing, you get a button that says I Made A Pig of Myself at Farrell's. My grandfather says maybe next time we go, he will make a pig of himself at Farrell's so the waiter can take a Polaroid picture of him and stick it up on the wall next to the picture of the guy from the next table.

My mom's friend Judy's dog had puppies and she invited us over to see them. They are so cute! She said she would give me one for keeps, but my mom said no.

I read 3 books - <u>The Truth About Mary Rose</u>, <u>Sister of the Bride</u>, and <u>The Fairy Doll</u>.

Our neighbor's house caught on fire but nobody died. My mom found out that the old man who lives there was smoking in bed!

I had a nice babysitter named Kim one night. My mom couldn't ask my grandparents because I'd been at their house all day and there was something at their church they wanted to go to with their friends. Kim is in 9th grade. She lives in my neighborhood. She did my hair and let me watch as much TV as I want. Her boyfriend's name is Brian. He is on the football team. He has a dog named Bear. Bear knows how to catch a Frisbee.

The End.

Kimberly invited me to her birthday party. I was the only white girl, and also the only girl from school.

The party was in a room at Lafayette Square, which is the mall where Kimberly's dad works. There wasn't much in there. Just a long table and a bunch of chairs. The cake was white with pink roses, but I let the girl sitting next to me have my rose coz store-bought icing gives me a headache. Kimberly's mom said I could have seconds of ice cream if I didn't like the cake. I didn't want to hurt her feelings so I lied and said it was delicious but I'm allergic.

We played a game where you had to stand over a milk bottle and drop a clothespin inside it and I won! The prize was a bottle of Blue Bonnet after-bath splash. It smells really good and comes in a bottle that looks like a flower.

There was a girl there named Jereena who loves Holly Hobby, same as me. She has the stationery and the sleeping bag and she gave Kimberly a Holly Hobby doll. We have the same favorite cartoon, too. Wheelie and the Chopper Bunch! We had a Soul Train dance line contest and Jereena won. She wrote her phone number down so my mom can call her mom to invite her over for a sleepover.

Guess what. Mrs. Voss threw up in the bathroom. Stacy N was waiting to use it and she heard.

We asked her how did she know for sure. Did it smell like throw up after? She said not really. That she could tell from the sound.

She made the sound for us. It kind of made me feel like throwing up to hear it.

If you throw up at school, you get to leave class and go to a little room next to the cafeteria where there's a cot to lie down on until your mom comes to pick you up.

Mrs. Voss didn't go lie down on the cot. She just walked back to her desk and told us to get out our math workbooks.

I think Stacy N was just trying to get attention.

Ginny made a secret club called Boycrazy Club. It's her, me, Lee Lindstrom, and Stacy Z. We each had to pick a boy to be in love with.

Lee picked Steven E.

Ginny picked Steven S coz him and Steven E are best friends and that makes her and Lee best friends, too.

Stacy picked Mr. Byrd! He is a 5th grade teacher and also coaches boys' sports.

When they asked me who I picked I said Jon Dorchen.

"Who's that?" Ginny said.

"A boy from my neighborhood," I said.

"Sorry," she told me, "It has to be a boy from school."

"Mr. Byrd's not a boy," I said. "He's a grown up."

Ginny looked at me like I was stupid and Stacy said it didn't matter, it just had to be someone from school so you could leave love notes in his cubby or the floor outside his classroom or someplace.

Lee asked did I want her to pick for me. I said okay, and she picked Jasper.

"You should've told her Jamie Craig," Ginny said.

Ginny's mean.

Ginny made a wedding dress store for Panther City. I wish I'd thought of that. I love drawing weddings.

Ginny said she and Lee are going to have a double wedding when they grow up.

Then at recess, she told Jasper I like him in front of everybody.

"Do not!" I said.

"Then why'd you tell me and Lee you do?" she said.

"I didn't," I said.

"Yes, she did," Stacy Z said. "I heard her!"

"Well, you like Mr. Byrd!" I told her.

"Look out, Jasper!" Ginny screamed. "Annie's gonna kiss you!"

She tried to push me on top of him, but I grabbed onto her dress and her pocket got ripped. She started crying even though it was her fault and yelling about how expensive her dress was and how when she tells her dad, he'll make my mom pay for it and if she doesn't, he'll sue.

"Shut up, Ginny!" I yelled. "I hate you and your stupid secret club!"

"What club?" Samantha asked. "Guys, what club?"

"Just some dumb club where people have to pick a boy to be in love with," I told her.

Samantha looked like she was about to cry. "Who all's in it?" she said.

"None of your beeswax!" I told her.

Steven S started wiggling his bottom at me. "Annie and Jasper sitting in a tree! K-I-S-S-I-N-G!"

"Shut up!" I yelled.

"What's going on over there?" Mrs. Voss shouted from the bench where she was sitting talking to one of the lunch ladies.

"First comes love!"

"If you don't like Jasper, then who do you like?" Lee asked.

"NO ONE!" I yelled.

Mrs. Voss stood up and started walking our way

"Then comes marriage!"

"She's probably a lezz," Ginny said.

"What's a lezz?" asked Kimberly.

"A lady who has sex with other ladies," Samantha whispered.

Everyone pointed and went "Awwwhhhmm!"

"STOP!" I screamed.

"You want to touch private parts with Jamie Craig!" Ginny yelled.

I grabbed her ponytail and yanked hard as I could. I know it hurt coz she screeched really loud. Mrs. Voss started to run.

Mrs. Voss says she's very disappointed in me, that I'm one of the ones she expects better from.

I tried to tell her it was Ginny's fault for making up all those lies about me, but she wouldn't listen. "Whatever anyone said or didn't say is immaterial," she said. "We do not hit. Ever."

"But the things she was saying were really dirty!" I said.

Mrs. Voss blew air out of her nostrils and looked at the ceiling. "What things?" she said.

I started crying coz I was too embarrassed to say. No matter how hard she tried to get me to tell her, I wouldn't.

"Okay," she said after a while and handed me a tissue.

My punishment is to stay inside for every recess this week.

And I have to stay at my desk. No Panther City HQ.

Someone wrote a bad word on Ginny's wedding dress store.

Now Ginny has to sit at her desk during every recess this week too for saying I'm the one who wrote that bad word on her store, when everyone knows it was Steven S. He's the only one who makes his letters backwards like a first grader.

Also, someone snuck into my cubby and dumped a full thingie of orange drink in my book bag and all the stuff that was inside of it got ruined!

"Girls, can you help me understand what's going on between the two of you?" Mrs. Voss asked.

"Nothing," I said.

"Nothing," Ginny said.

Jinx.

"It doesn't seem like nothing," Mrs. Voss said. "I thought the two of you were friends." She waited for one of us to say something, but we didn't. "Friends don't destroy each other's property," she said.

"I didn't destroy her property!" I yelled.

"Yes, you did!" Ginny yelled.

"You destroyed my book bag!"

"You destroyed my wedding dress store and you ripped the pocket off my brand new dress!"

"Okay, all right, you girls know what?" Mrs. Voss yelled. "I'm tabling this discussion. And changing your seating assignments!

Because I've just about HAD it with the way things are going around here. And if you don't shape up PDQ, there will be some other changes, changes you won't be too happy about. "

"I'm sorry," I said. To Mrs. Voss, not Ginny.

"Well, that's very nice," she said. "But I'd prefer you show me that through your actions."

Then she looked over at Ginny like "where's your apology?" But Ginny just gave a her a snotty look and fiddled with her Snoopy eraser. If I were Mrs. Voss I'd have taken that thing away from her for good!

Instead, she just said to go work on our math worksheets til the others got back from recess. Then she took a Coke can out of her desk, pulled the tab, and took a big drink, right in front of of us.

I raised my hand. "Mrs. Voss?" I said. "If we promise to be good and not fight, is it okay if we work on Panther City til the others get back?"

Mrs. Voss turned her head real slowly like "repetez, s'il-vous plâit?"

So I started to, but before I could finish, she shoved herself up from her chair so fast, her Coke spilled all over her desk. She didn't even clean it up, just rushed to the bathroom with her hand over her mouth.

I guess she had to go really bad…

Jasper's little sister died. Mrs. Voss said she decided to tell us in case we were wondering why he hadn't been in class lately. She asked could she count on all of us to be a good friend to him when he came back, and not tease or be mean.

"Lucky," Steven S whispered. "He gets to skip a whole week."

A bunch of us went to Panther City HQ and made tombstones with Jasper's little sister's name on them, to show him how sad we are.

Mrs. Voss said she appreciated the thought, but she didn't want us to make Jasper feel weird. "You can still hang them up. Everybody who made a tombstone, just flip it over and write a different name. Who here has been to a cemetery?"

I have! It's called Crown Hill. It's got a live deer who lives inside it. I've never seen the deer but Grampy and Mom have. Whenever we drive past Crown Hill, they tell me to look out the car window in case the deer is poking its head out of the fence.

Stacy N raised her hand. "Can we write funny names?" she asked.

Mrs. Voss said yes, as long as it didn't get out of hand.

Stacy Z raised her hand.

"Yes, Stacy?" Mrs. Voss said.

"My uncle Alan got a tattoo when he was in the Navy, and my grandma got really mad because it means he can't be buried when he dies."

"Why not?" Kimberly said.

"Because it's not allowed."

"That's dumb," Steven S said.

"You're dumb," Steven E said.

"I think that what Steven and Stacy are trying to say is that different religions believe different things," Mrs. Voss said.

"My Grandpa Smiley wants to be cremated!" Steven S said.

"What's that?" Kimberly said.

"It's when they put you in a big oven thing and burn you up til there's nothing left," Steven S said.

WHAT?! Everyone started talking and yelling at the same time.

"Class!" Mrs. Voss banged her desk and stuck her arm up. Hands up. Mouths shut. She told us that we had time for one more question, and then we had to move on. She looked around the room, trying to decide who to pick. I know she doesn't like when I wave my hand and go ooh ooh ooh, but I couldn't help it.

She picked Jamie Craig.

"My grandpa is buried in one of those marble houses with columns and a golden angel on top," he said. "They wrote his name in diamonds on the part underneath where the angel is."

Liar!

It's so unfair that she picked Liarbaby Jamie Craig instead of me! I was gonna ask if it was okay for me to make a deer for Panther City's cemetery.

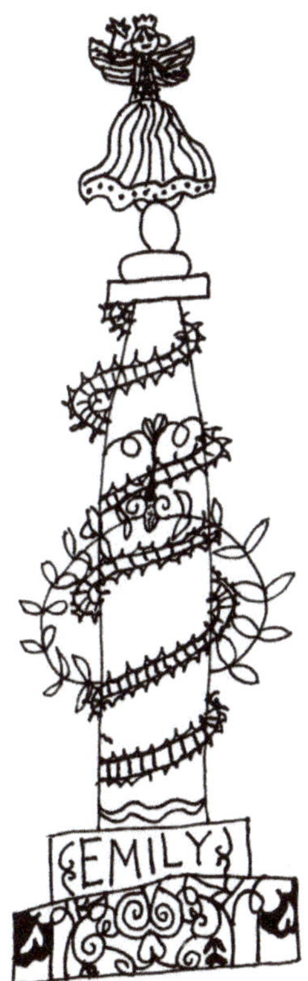

I asked Grampy did he want to get cremated like Steven S's grandpa and he said, "Heck no, I'd rather get my smoking done while I'm still around to enjoy it!" He raised his eyebrows like he does when he's being funny.

"Are you still messing with that imaginary town of yours?" he said.

"Yes," I said, "But Grampy, it's not a town, it's a city, and it's not imaginary, it's for school!"

"Is that right?" he said. He started futzing with his pipe. You have to suck on it really hard when you light the match or it won't start. "I've got an idea for it, if you want to hear."

"Okay," I said.

"It'll cost you."

"How much?"

"A hundred bucks."

"Grampy!" I yelled and smacked his arm.

"Okay, Squirt," he said, "This one's on the house, but after that, your credit's no good here."

"What's your idea?" I said.

He leaned back in the Bicentennial theme rocker Mom got him last Christmas and let the smoke leak out of his mouth up into his nostrils. "Cigar shop," he said. "Bet you dollars to doughnuts none of the other little kiddies have come up with that one yet!"

Even though I didn't like being called little kiddies, I got excited coz he was right!

"You can make an Indian chief to go outside of it," he said.

I asked him how come and he said that's how people know they've come to the right place. It's like the striped pole outside a barber shop. He said there's probably some other reason like the Indians trading the pilgrims tobacco for stuff like guns and beads, coz tobacco was the same as money for them. He asked did I ever read about that and I said no, but there's a part in <u>Little House on the Prairie</u> where two Indians come eat all Ma's cornbread and take Pa's tobacco so maybe that's how come people put Indian chief monuments outside of cigar stores.

LIQUOR
CHEAP BEER CHEAP BEER
ON SALE
LIQUOR &BEER
50% OFF
BEER BEER
BEER!
ICE

CIGARS
CIGARS

Panther
Pam's Roaring 70s
nude
XXX

MAY

We had a sub three days in a row. Her name was Miss Hastings and she wore a sweater that smelled like mothballs.

After we finished our work, we had to sit at our desks and do nothing. She wouldn't let us work on Panther City! We couldn't even read!

Steven Smiley told everyone her teeth were dentures.

Then he said her dentures were brown coz she liked sticking her tongue in people's buttholes and she heard him and smacked him hard right across the face.

Steven didn't say anything. He just went back to his desk and sat down. We waited for Miss Hastings to tell us something else to do, but she didn't, so we all just sat there til the bell rang to go home.

And the next day, instead of a substitute, we had Principal Moncrieff.

Lee Lindstrom raised her hand. "Excuse me, when is Mrs. Voss coming back?"

Principal Moncrieff clicked her fingernails on Mrs. Voss' Teacher of the Year award. It looks like an apple. Lee's mom collected money from the other moms, and gave it to her last Christmas with a card we all had to sign in secret.

"Mrs. Voss had an accident over the weekend, and after a lot of discussion, we've decided that it's in everyone's best interest for her to finish the rest of the year out at home."

Everybody started talking at once.

"What happened to her?"

"Was she in a car crash?"

"Was she drunk?"

"No, she wasn't drunk," Principal Moncrieff snapped. "And you may spend the next hour in the hall, Steven Smiley, thinking about what sort of boy would make such a tasteless joke."

He wasn't joking. He was just asking. Everybody knows he used to have three brothers but one of them got drunk and crashed his motorcycle and now he's only got two.

"If anyone has anything to contribute with regard to their schoolwork, they may do so by raising their hands like ladies and gentlemen," Principal Moncrieff said. "However, I'll not be answering any questions having to do with Mrs. Voss or her private business. Anyone who cares to speculate will find themselves out in the hall alongside Mr. Smiley."

Heather raised her hand and asked if we had to have Miss Hastings as our sub again. Principal Moncrieff said no, that she would be taking charge of us until a new teacher could be found.

Kimberly raised her hand and asked if we could make cards for Mrs. Voss. Principal Moncrieff said yes, that that was a lovely idea, provided we finished all of our schoolwork first.

I raised my hand. "Can we work on Panther City after we're finished with our cards?"

"No," Principal Moncrieff said, "I'm declaring that project finished as of today. It's time you start exploring the solar system."

When we came in the next day, Panther City was gone.

PANTHER CITY

Teacher's Edition

©1973

SEPTEMBER

"**G**ood bunch?" he asked his wife over dinner. His appetite for chatter about the children in her class was finite, but today had been the first full day of school, and last year, her first, had been a roughie. He knew to at least make a show of interest.

She chewed, swallowed, and gave a conditional nod. "I think so. No overt nutballs, anyway."

"No…what was that kid's name again?"

"Which kid?" She knew, of course, and felt that Richard should have, too.

"Last year. The big guy with the bowl haircut."

"They've all got that haircut," she said. It was 1973.

"The one who kept pushing everybody off the jungle gym."

"Kenny Buntz," she relented

"Kenny Buntz! Who got stuck with him this year?"

"Cathy."

Cathy was a legend, tough, but fair, a battle-hardened vet who insisted she didn't care if the children liked her. All the parents wanted Cathy for fourth grade. Cathy knew what she was doing. If anyone could whip Kenny Buntz into shape, it was her.

"That kid ran circles around you," Richard observed, spearing another piece of chicken.

It hurt to admit, but he was right. And Kenny had not been an isolated case, merely the worst of a bad bunch. That's the phrase the more experienced teachers had thrown around, when they encountered her weeping in the faculty room.

Buntz, Kistling, Staub… out of student earshot, the teachers batted those names around freely, let it all hang out. Somehow, though, her colleagues' anecdotes always ended with them getting the better of those tough nuts, making her feel even worse. When her contract was renewed at the end of the year, it felt as if a mistake had been made.

"So who's your favorite this year?" Richard asked.

"Rich, it's the first day."

"What was her name, last year, the good one?"

"Angela."

"Angela!" Richard helped himself to another roll. "Who's this year's Angela?"

"I don't… It's not like… I don't want to be one of those teachers who automatically slaps on petty labels without even bothering to… You know, good kid, bad kid, troublemaker…"

"Yeah, but I bet you know." He aimed his fork at her like a hunter sighting his rifle and waggled it until she smiled back.

"Ok, first impressions? They seem like a much better bunch."

"That's my girl! Another year like last one, and I'd be carting you off to the loony bin."

"Ha ha." She shot him a sour look.

"You think I'm being funny? Those little criminals made my woman cry!"

"They're not 'little criminals'. They're children. And yeah, maybe they were a bad bunch, but I was their teacher. It's not their fault I let them get to me."

She was ashamed of her peevish tone. She should feel lucky to have such a supportive husband. He was trying to make her laugh, and here she was, acting like an ungrateful little brat, tossing her wadded up napkin onto her plate, voice shaking.

"Annie, come on."

She glared in defiance.

Pushing his chair back with a sigh, he came to squat alongside her. With his arm around her shoulders he touched his forehead to her temple. "Listen to me, ok? You're a great teacher and those kids are lucky to have you."

She retrieved her napkin, and put it in her lap. "Ok. Thanks. Can we please just change the subject?"

JANUARY

The idea of making a city grew from a conversation with her college roommate. The last time they'd talked had been early December, when Joanne had her in stitches, describing the over-the-top Thanksgiving pageant her sister, Tammy, had staged with her Sunday school class.

Now that the holidays were behind them, Tammy and her Sunday school kids were busy constructing a model of Jerusalem, a task that required Joanne to choke down copious quantities of V8. According to Joanne, Tammy thought the cans resembled watchtowers such as might have existed in the Holy Land, once upon a time. "The kids are supposed to be bringing them in, but y'know, it's just Sunday school. And they're what, five? If it were me, I'd stick with felt boards and coloring pages, but you know Tammy. She's always got to put the big pot in the little, get all handicrafty."

"I still can't picture what she's doing with those V8 cans."

"I told you! Watchtowers! In case the Romans invade or something. You should hear all the trash she's got them hauling in! Margarine tubs, pipe cleaners, popsicle sticks–"

"Yeah, but what are they doing with them to make them look … Are they going to paint them, or–"

"Why are you asking me? I just drink the V8! Not to be sacrilegious, but it's probably gonna look like crap. Who cares? They're five."

"You know, it could be fun to do something like that with my kids. We're about to start an urban study unit."

"I'm not drinking any more V8."

"Yeah, no, that part sounds like a hassle, but it wouldn't have to be 3-D. You could make the whole thing out of construction paper, like a collage. We've got three big bulletin boards along the back wall. And the kids love anything that's hands on. Could be a fun way to spark their interest. I am so sick of stupid worksheets, having them take turns reading aloud from the textbook–"

"Why not? You're kind of crafty, right?"

"Yeah, but this wouldn't be about me. The kids would be the ones doing the work. That's how they learn. I mean, I'd probably have to clear it with the principal if it's the kind of thing that takes more than a day or two, but I really like the idea of them working on something together, having the satisfaction of watching something you're working on take shape. A couple of those kids are really good artists, too. Seriously. I wish you could see. I've got some real smarties this year."

"You really love those little brats, don't you?"

"I do."

"That's why I want you and Rich to get crackin' on one of your own!"

"How about you let me put my degree to use first?"

"Unnghh… okay, whatever you say, Teach."

In anticipation of the project's start, she covered all three bulletin boards with a couple of rolls of festive yellow paper. She'd hoped for a mix of grey, green, and blue, to suggest asphalt, grass and sky, but yellow was the only option the faculty supply closet had in sufficient quantity. And given the disrespectful way last year's bunch had treated her decorations, she'd stopped dipping into her own pocket to make her classroom nice.

"Boys and girls, you may be wondering why our bulletin boards look so empty," she said. "What if I tell you that we're going to fill them up with a city you'll design yourselves, working together, using your imaginations as tools?"

The children needed no convincing, all of them yammering away at the same time, neglecting to raise their hands.

"What's its name gonna be?"

"Can it be like the one in <u>The Wizard of Oz</u>?"

"Can it be for cats, not people?"

Their enthusiasm was exhausting, but she'd learned how to stay on top of it, not letting the swells of manic energy swamp her, as they had last year. There'd been a learning curve, of course. But four months in, she was pretty sure of what to expect from this bunch.

Half the girls would want to copy Lee Lindstrom. Lee was a natural leader, the extremely bright child of parents with high expectations, pretty, athletic, already reading well above grade level. At some point, the girls would have to start thinking for themselves, but for now, she was content to let Lee determine their course. Maybe somewhere down the road, they could have a talk about supply and demand, discuss whether or not their city could support half a dozen pet stores.

When it came to the boys, Steven Smiley was the one to keep tabs on. He looked like Dennis the Menace, but some of the things she'd heard coming out of that mouth were as raunchy as anything on Rich's beloved Richard Pryor records. He wasn't a bad kid, just feral, popular, and more invested in distracting his classmates than completing his schoolwork. He had an older brother who drove a Camaro and a mother who was almost old enough to be his grandmother…

But no Kenny Buntzes. No Kistlings, no Staubs…

She couldn't help herself from going on and on about the children's adorable first efforts. Watching them labor over every little building, then carefully choose where to stick it on the bulletin board was surprisingly rewarding. Maybe she was a good teacher after all.

"Promise you'll come see it in person," she begged at dinner, overlooking Rich's clear lack of interest. "Seriously, babe, I'm not doing it justice."

Dear Families,

Class 3B has been working very hard on
the city we've been"building" on our
classroom's bulletin boards. I look
forward to showing you this work-in-
progress on Parents Night.

I am afraid that some of the magazines
the children have brought in from home
have contained pictures that are not
appropriate for school or this age
group, so from now on, please limit
your contributions to wrapping paper,
any leftover wallpaper you may have,
greeting cards, and catalogues (no
underwear pictures please.)

Thanks in advance for your
understanding.

Mrs. Voss

Class 3B

One of the kids – Annie – almost fell to pieces when informed she'd have to cover the word 'Indianapolis' on the facade of her building, a reasonable facsimile of <u>The Indianapolis Star</u>'s boxy, red brick headquarters on the way to the Circle downtown. Her mother worked for <u>The Star</u>'s Women's pages, apparently. Mrs. Voss had been a bit hard pressed to follow what the girl was saying through her tears. Something about brides and dogs.

Live and learn. Next year, she'd sidestep this type of situation by having the class name its city from the get go.

Maybe she'd tweak the process by which the name was selected, too.

Richard was going to die when he heard the kids' first choice of name. The teachers who were in the faculty room at lunch had nearly wet themselves when she told them. Chocolate City. The utter obliviousness of third graders. Innocence, really. So cute.

Had they gone with Chocolateville or Chocolatesburg, there would have been no issue, but unfortunately the faculty room harbored a rat, and word of Chocolate City spread fast. Before she had finished her Sprite, the principal bustled in like some malevolent Mrs. Tiggywinkle, telling her she'd have to change the name to something less provocative. Characteristically, she provided zero guidance on how to frame the underlying reason for this decision to a roomful of 8-year-olds, one of whom happened to be Black.

In the end, Mrs. Voss kept her manner no nonsense, like the pantyhose. The kids had been disappointed, but there'd been very little pushback. She focused their attention on reconstructing the list she'd erased from the board. "Come on, guys. We don't have all day to spend on this."

The kids wanted to know if they could submit new candidates along with their original suggestions.

She told them yes, if they felt they must. It was the least she could do. That goddamn principal.

The new suggestions were about what you'd expect. Wackypackopolis. Dallascowboysnumberonetown. Sprawling compounds that looked utterly nonsensical written out.

Panther City had been Kimberly's idea. Bless her heart. She was a cool customer, that one, her bookish wire rim glasses a marked contrast from the colorful plastic barrettes her mother clipped to the tips of her braids. She offered no explanation as to her choice, and Mrs. Voss didn't inquire.

Like Chocolate City before it, Panther City won by a landslide.

Mrs. Moncrieff couldn't possibly object. Not when the school mascot was a panther. A black one.

Parkview Country Day Power!

The girls, the girls! They were driving her out of her gourd. Their petty competition, their bossiness, their never-ending feuds and accusations.

Rough as they were, the boys were far more manageable. With the exception of Jamie Craig, who was intelligent but whiny, an irritant to his classmates and, if she were being honest, herself, they weren't nearly as fixated on the dynamics of Panther City. Given a choice of how to spend their time, they might pick it over quiet reading, but it was nothing compared to the joys of chasing each other around the playground in their slippery jackets and enormous pom-pom hats – silver and blue for the Cowboys, turquoise and orange for the Dolphins.

Next to the girls, the boys were practically Neanderthals. That was natural enough. The science said they developed more slowly, mentally and emotionally. Not all of them, of course. Steven Epstein was a real history buff, who grasped mathematical concepts as soon as they were introduced.

Steven E was a pleasure to have in class but her absolute favorite was Jasper Burns, a smart, self-contained boy who applied himself to his schoolwork, held his own at recess, and was every bit the artist as Annie or Lee Lindstrom.

Jasper was this year's Angela.

Sometimes teaching seemed like a vocation. Other times the whole enterprise felt as blah as the TV dinners she pulled from the freezer after a particularly trying day, shamefully aware that Cathy never subjected her husband to such a disappointing meal.

The field trip to the Statehouse had been an abject bust.

Maybe Rich was right that she was running herself ragged for no reason. Why put the big pot in the little, as Joanne would say. Her elaborate attempts to demonstrate what a creative, fun teacher she was were hardly ever worth the effort, leaving her wiped out and cranky.

The energy she'd expended on that Statehouse trip, organizing permission slips and transportation, lining up chaperones, making nice with lunch ladies who did not hide their resentment at being asked to provide sack lunches…

And then? The children couldn't have been more bored. It had been painful to watch. Stacy Nelson's mother hadn't even pretended to pay attention to the docent, rummaging through her giant handbag like a raccoon. Some chaperone!

She also felt like stabbing whatever Roman senator had decided a circular marble atrium should be called a "rotunda." Why not a nipple or an anus? God only knew what the docent, a starchy blue hair with pearl earrings, a Pendleton kilt and a jaw like a marionette's, had thought about the children after they heard that. Steven Smiley had been so jacked up, she'd had to hold his hand like a kindergartner's. It was humiliating.

Jasper's mother, her other chaperone, tried to minimize their misbehavior on the ride back to school. Mrs. Voss recognized this for an attempt to make her feel better, but the fact that Jasper had merely smiled his Mona Lisa smile while the rest of the class jumped around like monkeys, howling, "Rotunda! Rotunda!" made his mother's observation that "boys will be boys" a touch disingenuous.

"Don't let the girls off the hook," she told her. She hoped this didn't come off as unfriendly, but she'd exhausted her capacity for small talk, and needed to concentrate on Steven Smiley's turquoise and orange pom-pom poking up from the seat directly behind the driver's. She'd forced him to sit there, while the other boys raced to the back. "Your son is an absolute pleasure, by the way."

"Well," Mrs. Burns smiled, "He's always had an interest in government, so this trip was right up his alley. Believe me, he can put up quite a squawk when I tell him it's time to turn off The Six Million Dollar Man and do his homework."

Mrs. Voss produced a polite chuckle. She wished Jasper's mother had seated herself next to Stacy N's.

"I do worry about leaning on him too much," Mrs. Burns continued, lowering her voice. "I don't want him looking back on this time and feeling he missed out."

"Jasper always participates fully."

"Oh, I know that," his mother agreed. "He's always been my little soldier…" Her eyes welled.

Jamie Craig gave a wail as his silver and blue Dallas Cowboys
cap sailed up the aisle.

"Excuse me," Mrs Voss snapped, launching herself toward
the back of the bus.

Whichever little ruffian had necessitated her intervention
with this violation, she owed him for providing such a
convenient conversational out.

FEBRUARY

History was threatening to repeat itself. She was losing control of her classroom again. The children had no respect for themselves, their work, each other or her. The obscene drawing that had appeared on Steven Epstein's drive-in movie screen was proof.

The legendary Cathy was quick to tell her where she'd erred. "I'd have made sure there was a movie on that screen before he put it up, even if he had to make one up. Blank space is just asking for it. Except in art class. Then they're all like "Wahhh, I don't know what to draw!" What is it, anyway? A wang dang doodle?"

"No, um…" Mrs. Voss gestured vaguely to her own chest.

"Ah so! Boobies. Always a crowdpleaser. Who's the perp?"

Mrs. Voss had an idea, but she was weary of playing Grasshopper to Cathy's Master Po. Shrugging, she claimed that she was mystified as to when the vandal, whoever he was, would have found the opportunity."

"Anne. Listen to yourself. There's how many of them and how many of you? It was probably a coordinated effort. You know, one guy's the look out and another one creates a distraction, so the third guy can make off with the jewels."

"A side of me is wondering if maybe it wasn't Samantha Accardi. Her mother's a–"

"Sex doctor, I know."

"I was going to say marriage counselor."

"Whatever she is, she should teach her kid to shut up about it. If she were my daughter? There'd be a bar of soap in that mouth so fast, bubbles would come out her nose!"

"I don't know, maybe it's healthy. That she's not ashamed."

"Right, which is why it wasn't her. Why make a dirty drawing if you don't think it's dirty? Were I to hazard a guess, I'd pin it on that little blondie."

"Steven Smiley? Yeah," Mrs. Voss admitted. "Me too." Way to go, Ironside.

"That kid's what I call a real live wire. Can't really hate him for it, though. He's like–

"Please don't say Dennis the–"

"Dennis the Menace."

Mrs. Voss put her head in her hands.

"Know what I'd do, in your shoes?" Cathy offered. "Tell 'em that's it. No more Panther City."

"I did do that! They made me so mad I couldn't see straight."

"Good!"

"No! Not good at all. If you'd have seen their faces? Half the girls were in tears."

"Oh, boo hoo, cry me a river. Ever hear of this little thing called consequences?"

"It's just so … arbitrary, punishing all of them for the crimes of one or two."

"Honey, use your head. You don't <u>really</u> do it. You just tell them you're going to. Let 'em twist in the wind a bit. Then, when all hope is lost, you swoop in and announce that you've decided to give them one more chance."

"I don't know, that seems a little… maybe it <u>is</u> time we move on from Panther City."

"Sure, but not like this. They'd hate you for it."

"I'm not sure what they're even getting from it anymore."

"What, you mean is it educational?"

Mrs. Voss nodded, miserably.

"Forgive me for telling it like it is, but get a grip! Their workbooks? The mimeographs? That's what's educational. The rest is just yummies. This Panther City stuff? Personally, it's not my style, but you should feel proud of yourself for coming up with it. It's a freebie, basically. They stay busy. You get a rest. Everybody wins. You want to take that away, fine, but you'd best know what you're doing."

"That's the problem. I don't. I really don't."

"I know you don't," Cathy said. "But I do. And if you're being smart, you'll listen."

Richard's visit to the classroom was a huge hit, of course. He had that effect on people, generally speaking.

It was no mystery why they picked on Jamie Craig. That smug little face. How readily he cried. His inability to see how claiming he had an Olympic-sized swimming pool in his back yard only intensified his peers' disdain.

When they called him a liar, he doubled down, insisting he was permitted to fly a private plane his father most certainly did not own. That his pet dog's collar was studded with diamonds. That his family had a castle in Switzerland. A bottomless fountain of pig shit, as Richard would say.

She frequently fantasized about telling Jamie to shut up. Instead, she was obligated to punish Kevin Dupree and Steven S for knocking the wind out of him on the playground, benching them until they apologized. Privately, she felt Jamie reaped what he sowed. He was insufferable.

MARCH

Too late, Mrs. Voss realized that she'd erred by letting "fun" businesses proliferate unchecked. Pet stores, ice cream parlors, tutu "shoppes" – no wonder the kids clashed. Third grade taxonomy held that anything related to animals, toys, or sweets was a prize to be hotly desired.

But a working city was more than just commerce. There was infrastructure, too, roads and telephone poles and all manner of civil engineering projects.

Sadly, such initiatives proved tricky to render. A number of female Panther citizens had gone apoplectic over the "lampposts" she'd charged some of the more recalcitrant boys with making. "They're making our city ugly on purpose!"

The boys, gratified by the girls' response, upped their production.

For years, her in-laws had celebrated their wedding anniversary with dinner at the King Cole. There were any number of nice restaurants closer to their home on the far Northside, but the King Cole was their tradition. A tradition she'd been expected to participate in, ever since she'd gotten involved with their son.

The elder Vosses also insisted on carpooling, so as not to waste money parking two vehicles downtown. She'd floated the idea of paying for valet parking as their anniversary gift, but Rich, detecting a barbed edge just below the proposal's surface, said no.

"I didn't mean we should drive separately," she dissembled. "I meant we could take one car, let the guy park it, and all go in together, rather than the driver having to drop everyone off, then walk a half mile back to the restaurant. Especially when your mom's so jumpy about…being downtown."

Rich shot her a look. "My dad's loyal to his lot from back when his office was down on Delaware. It's only a problem if you make it one."

They wound up taking Rich's car. Bill expressed his desire that it should be parked in his preferred lot as soon as he had settled into the passenger seat his daughter-in-law made a show of giving up for him.

She hated sitting in back, a prisoner to her mother-in-law's conversation and her nauseating clouds of Shalimar. "This block used to be lovely before urban blight," Myrna sighed as they drew closer to their destination. "It makes me ashamed," she growled two minutes later, "All this urban blight." A block later, a couch on a sagging porch inspired her to remark, "If that doesn't say 'urban blight', I don't know what does."

The younger Mrs. Voss dug her nails into her palms to keep from screaming at the thinness of the euphemism. When they pulled up outside the restaurant, she refused to get out. "I'm feeling kind of queasy," she told them. "A couple blocks of fresh air will do me good."

"Darling, no!" Myrna had cried, making a shooing motion at the uniformed Black valet. "Come wait inside with us. We'll get a drink in you. That'll settle your stomach."

"Thanks, but actually, I'd prefer to walk with my husband," she countered, climbing decisively back in front.

"What's up with you?" Richard asked, as they pulled away.

"Didn't you hear me say I'm feeling kind of urpy? I think I'm allergic to some chemical in your mother's perfume."

"Jesus, Annie!" he exploded. "Can we not?"

"What? I'm serious! It happens whenever I'm shut up in a moving car with her!"

"Unbelievable." Rich shook his head and hung a hard right.

The car reeked of Shalimar, vinyl upholstery, and coats that had gone all winter without drying cleaning. The cumulative effect suddenly conspired to make her feel urpy for real.

"Rich, pull over," she commanded, grappling with the door handle. "Hurry! I'm gonna barf!"

He wrenched the wheel to the curb, as she hung out the door, spattering it with her stomach contents.

His testiness evaporated immediately. One hand rubbed her between the shoulder blades while the other rummaged in her purse for the tissue pack she kept there. "What do you want to do?" he asked after a minute. "They're waiting."

"I just need to sit a bit," she gasped, too ashamed to ask if there had been any witnesses. Thank god the area was virtually deserted after 5 o'clock. "You don't have to stay with me. Go park the car."

"What if you need to throw up again?"

"I'm fine. I just needed to get that crap out of my stomach."

"I don't think I should leave you here."

"Rich, it's fine. It's not even that dark yet! Ditch the car, then come find me. Look, there's a bench. I'll be right there."

"We could go back to the restaurant. I could run in and tell them we need to reschedule. I'm sure they'd understand."

"I don't want to spoil their anniversary for them."

She was both pleased and disappointed when he nodded and drove off. Wait til Myrna learned her son had left his bride so undefended against the horrors of urban blight.

The bench she waited on was positioned along the perimeter

of a treeless park, directly across from a statue of some long ago dignitary. Dead for a hundred years, probably. She squinted at the name carved into the plinth. Benjamin Harrison. The same as the fort. He'd been president at some point, she didn't know when. She squinted at the inscription. Like so many of those founding father types he'd worn a lot of hats. Lawyer, publicist, brigadier general, senator…she wondered if he was any relation to William Henry Harrison, the sole president to be born in Indiana, who caught a cold at his own inauguration and died a month later.

History.

When was the last time anybody'd bothered to read this plinth? Years probably.

To hell with lampposts. Maybe what Panther City needed was some monuments. The prospect was invigorating.

As was the prospect of a big expensive King Cole steak.

It turned out she was pregnant.

Her mother-in-law crowed that she'd suspected as much.

Chance encounters with students and parents were a hazard of the job, one she tried to avoid whenever possible, even if it meant staying in her parked car or ducking into Woolworth's 'til the coast was clear.

When cornered, she felt no guilt about inventing a pressing engagement to justify a swift exit.

How could all those parents fail to realize that the supermarket or Glendale Mall were not appropriate locations to discuss a student's classroom performance, especially with said student standing right there? Last year, a mother with son in tow had waylaid her in the feminine hygiene aisle of Hook's Drugs.

Jasper's mother was too discreet to ever pull such a stunt. Still, Mrs. Voss wished she'd noticed her in time to give her the slip, rather than simultaneously converging on Calico Corners' cutting table, bolts in arms.

Jasper's mother tapped Mrs. Voss's selection, an old-fashioned cotton print of teddies and alphabet blocks. "How precious. What's it for?"

"A crib quilt," Mrs. Voss tossed off, in a tone meant to discourage follow up questions.

"I'm sure it'll be darling." Jasper's mother's finger traced one of the teddy bears, as her eyes filled with tears.

Mrs. Voss, remembering the field trip to the State Capital,

dug for her tissue pack. "I'm sorry," Jasper's mother snuffled. "I'm just coming from the hospital. I don't know if Jasper has shared what's going on with his sister."

He hadn't, though it soon became clear why he was Panther City's resident expert on hospital operations. Mrs. Burns provided a timeline. A healthy, cheerful baby, her husband's longed for girl…a delightful toddler…then a stubborn cold, lingering lethargy…a visit to the pediatrician …tests…more tests…a rare form of cancer…various promising treatments implemented without success…prayers….neighbors pitching in to provide dinner and feed the dog… grandparents flying in from Florida and Arizona…

"I'm so sorry," Mrs. Voss said awkwardly. "I had no idea. If there's anything I can do…"

The lone saleswoman bustled toward the cutting table, chirping apologies for having gotten herself stuck behind the register. Jasper's red-eyed mother gestured that Mrs. Voss should go first. Teddy bears and alphabet blocks flopped the length of the cutting table as the saleswoman glanced up from her shears, smiling conspiratorially.

"Are congratulations in order, Mommy?"

The kids weren't the only ones counting the hours 'til spring vacation. Five days in Sarasota with her husband sounded like a perfect escape.

Richard's parents had offered to pay for their flights, which made the cost of their hotel room feel less extravagant. It wasn't on the beach, but it had a pool. She planned to bask next to it until the Florida sunshine leeched away every bit of stress related to origami paper, X-rated drive-in movie screens, and those awful candy dots the kids picked from long paper strips they smuggled into their laps.

"Hubba hubba, Britt Ekland," Richard growled when she modeled her new bathing suit for him in the living room. It hadn't dawned on him that this might be the last two-piece of her life.

This time next year, their baby would be on the outside. It was pretty much all she thought about. She found herself compulsively humming "Three is a Magic Number" from those funny Schoolhouse Rock cartoons. Three was a serious one, though, so hauntingly beautiful, it made her cry.

Schoolhouse Rock did a much better job of teaching multiplication tables than she did. She admitted it! She wasn't proud.

Or rather, she wasn't as proud as Cathy. Yet. She'd get there. Maybe.

APRIL

Before round-the-clock morning sickness wreaked havoc with her vacation, she'd imagined returning to the classroom tanned, rested, and ready to educate those kids' brains out.

Now, she dreamed of quitting.

Richard wanted her to. Not right away, of course. Contractually, she was obligated to finish out the year.

Her pregnancy was still a secret. She wasn't showing yet. The children barely seemed to notice how she had to abandon her desk a couple of times a day, right in the middle of a lesson. Her fear was not making it to the bathroom in time, or that she might find it occupied upon arrival. Some of the kids took forever to do their business in there.

The handful of friends she'd confided in assured her the queasiness would abate soon.

Her job struck them as a no-brainer. "Take a couple years off. Enjoy that baby! Have another! You can always go back once the little one starts nursery school."

Rich said the same. They didn't really _need_ her income. He was working his way up the ladder, earning good money. Did she honestly think of teaching as a vocation, the way it so clearly was for someone like Cathy?

Maybe she could open a gift shop or something.

"Hey, Mrs. V!" her old nemesis, Kenny Buntz yelled, as Cathy's class passed hers in the hall, one group heading to French, the other to gym.

Cathy drew up short at this transgression, bringing the entire column of fourth graders to a halt as she glared down the line from her position at its head. Kenny, already tall for his age, had been held back in second grade, so her view was unobstructed. Her eyes drilled into his as she raised a finger to her lips. Kenny mirrored the gesture without hesitation or apparently, hard feelings. Cathy faced forward and the line forged silently ahead.

Amazing. Kenny Buntz had been tamed.

Mrs. V. It had a gratifyingly chummy ring.

He'd never called her that before.

None of them had.

Ginny Schmidt's snub-nosed, freckle-chested mother called the principal, livid at how the skirmish between her daughter and Annie had been handled.

It made Mrs. Voss' blood boil. How dare that awful woman go straight to the administration? Had she raised her concern in a phone call or note, Mrs. Voss would have been more than happy to discuss the matter with her.

Perhaps someone should tell Mrs. Schmidt her spoiled youngest was far from the innocent victim she was making her out to be. Mrs. Voss was well acquainted with the type. She'd had a Ginny of her own in elementary school. Rebecca Norris. The adults thought she was all sugar and spice, but Mrs. Voss was wise to her true nature. Girls like Rebecca and Ginny were venomous pot-stirrers, spreading baseless rumors, pitting friend against friend. Nothing was ever their fault. Rebecca's father had been a prominent lawyer, too, a fact she lorded over the others, just like Ginny.

What she wouldn't give to show Mrs. Schmidt the sheet of origami paper on which her blameless angel had rated the other girls' attractiveness on a scale of 1 to 5, deliberately leaving it atop Panther City HQ's scrap pile for the others to find. Mrs. Voss had whisked it away, burying it all the way at the bottom of the garbage. She prayed that Kimberly and Samantha would never get wind of their scores. Ginny had awarded herself second place. Not even she dared rank herself above Lee Lindstrom.

Darling Ginny had also dumped a cupful of water on Jamie

Craig, so as to accuse him of wetting his pants, getting him so worked up that he did, a little bit.

As if her job wasn't exhausting enough!

Was it really so unreasonable to expect her principal to stick up for her, just a little bit? Maybe this was the norm at other schools. At Parkview Country Day, the principal belonged to the same country club as the parents.

Ginny was the fifth Schmidt child to be entrusted to Parkview. They were, Mrs. Moncrieff told Mrs. Voss, a wonderful family. The older children were all active in their fraternities and sororities. It had been wonderful catching up with them when they were home for their Christmas break. The boy closest in age to Ginny excelled at tennis to such a degree, he would probably qualify for an athletic scholarship, not that they needed it. When it came to Mrs. Schmidt's selfless volunteer history, enough good could not be said. And Mr. Schmidt could always be counted on for a generous donation, no matter the cause.

The deck was stacked, in other words. Mrs. Voss wished she could rip the pockets off the entire clan. Let 'em sue. She didn't care.

L ong distance was an expensive indulgence, but worth it, she thought, twining the phone cord around her wrist like Marie Antoinette. Joanne really listened to her, exhibiting far more insights and patience than she ever had in college. She didn't trivialize her concerns like Richard. When Mrs. Voss complained to him about Ginny Schmidt's mother, he suggested taking her mind off it with a shopping trip. It was maddening!

"That woman should thank her lucky stars I didn't land her daughter's bony butt in the principal's office. Not that it would have mattered. They're in cahoots, those two. I swear to you, Jo, had you seen the way those kids were going at each other– scratching, pulling each other's hair, ripping each other's pockets off–"

"Ye gods! What started it?"

"Who knows? The one's kid's a spoiled b-i-t-c-h to begin with, but the other, I don't know. Do you remember me telling you about that city they've been making?"

"Excuse me, you're welcome. I seem to recall being the one to give you the idea!"

"Oh duh, right, Tammy's Sunday school."

"All that V8 I drank?"

"They haven't sainted you for that, yet?"

"Unfortunately not."

"Well, okay, so the other kid is really territorial about the stupid city, so that's probably– wait, what are you eating?"

"Pringles. Is the sound of them driving you crazy? I can stop if it's activating your morning sickness or something."

"It's activating my appetite is what it's activating! If I could crawl through phone lines, I'd be ripping that can out of your paws and stuffing them in my mouth right now!"

"See, that's why I hate you and Rich having moved to India-NO-place so much. If you were closer, I could run to IGA and buy you all the Pringles you want. Special delivery."

"Don't make me cry."

"No crying! I want to hear more about the little b-i-t-c-h."

"Ugh, where to start? To be fair, it's not just her. It's the whole herd. They act like they're possessed."

"Like that kid in <u>The Exorcist!</u> Your mother sucks cocks in hell!"

"What?"

"You didn't see it?

"Me? Of course not. Anyway, the one with the mother? Empties an entire carton of orange drink in the territorial one's book bag because of someone writing 'POOP' on her bridal salon."

Joanne howled.

"It's funny but not. Remember last year, how some kids tore up all my classroom decorations?"

"I know, but c'mon! Poop?"

"I'm being serious. Would you like it if everyone disrespected your authority? Every time I turn my back, they're doing stuff to each other's buildings or stealing each other's origami paper or sneaking behind the bushes to make up X-rated stories or–"

"What!?"

"Ugh, forget it." Her mood was souring fast. "This whole city thing was fun at first but now it just feels like a fiasco. I hate it! I should just pull the plug and be done with it."

"So, why don't you?"

"I don't know. I was talking to this other teacher. She made it seem like they'd hate me for it. That it wouldn't be fair."

"Okay well, what if you pull the plug on that job instead?"

"That's what Rich wants."

"What do you want?"

"I don't know. That, maybe."

"Know what I'd do if I were you?" Joanne munched and swallowed, drawing out the suspense. "I'd tell the brass I'd been put on bed rest, effective immediately."

"I'm not that far along."

"They don't know that! If they don't know you're pregnant, how are they gonna know when you're due? In those frumpy jean jumpers? You could be giving birth tomorrow."

"Gee, thanks."

"Seriously, just march yourself into that horrible principal's office and say, "Listen up, sister, there's a bun in this here oven and if I don't follow doctor's orders, you're gonna have a bunch of third graders drowning in amniotic fluid, so how about you get on the horn and find yourself a substitute?" Do you know what her car looks like?"

"The principal's? Buick, I think. It's a big old boat."

"Great. So, get yourself a can of spray paint and on your way out out of Dodge, write 'POOP' on her hood. Make it stick."

J asper had been out for a week, and Mrs. Voss was
wrestling with what to tell her class. In the end, she told
them the truth, and that she was depending on them to
treat him with extra kindness, as it was surely a very sad time
for him. The girls rose to the occasion, raiding their Panther
City supply stash to make homemade sympathy cards she
could not, in good conscience, let them give Jasper, though
she appreciated the thought.

She and Rich had both liked the name Emily, though they
couldn't have one now, obviously. She liked the sound of
Jasper, too, but that would be weird, to name a baby Jasper
right after you'd had a Jasper in class. Rich wasn't keen on it
anyway, said it sounded like some kind of flowering shrub.

She'd much rather dwell on baby names than the odds of
having your baby sicken and die on you.

Nor did she want to spend much time thinking of what to
say in a sympathy note to that child's grieving mother.
Maybe she could get away with signing a pretty card.

MAY

The teachers received mimeographs, informing them that a small delegation from The Indiana Association of School Principals would be visiting the school between 10:00 and noon. Mrs. Moncrieff would be escorting them to select classrooms. The children should continue to engage in their activities as usual. The visiting principals didn't want to cause a disruption. Their purpose was merely to observe.

They hit her room at quiet reading time, to find the children ranged around the room, some at their desks, others sprawled comfortably on the rug. Annie, Jasper, and Jamie Craig were stationed at Panther City HQ. She rose to greet the visitors, then returned to the math quizzes she'd been grading at her desk on the assumption that she, too, was being observed. It felt like she was putting on a performance. The children, too. They barely moved, modeling the sort of studiousness that doesn't scratch, stretch or turn so much as a page.

The visitors were all female save one, who drifted over to Panther City HQ, where he peered over Jamie Craig's shoulder with an approving nod. Mrs. Voss and the other kids watched surreptitiously as Jamie, puffed up on attention, ferried his newest department store to the bulletin boards. The visitor trailed behind, crouching to inspect the placement after Jamie selected a location near the bottom and moved on.

"Good lord!" he exclaimed, rocking back on his heels so forcefully, he nearly lost his balance. Mrs. Moncrieff had already started herding the rest of the group toward the door. He had to scramble to rejoin them.

The children dissolved in giggles as soon as the door closed behind the visitors. Mrs. Voss had to raise her voice to be heard. "Boys and girls, we have five more minutes of quiet reading time. I expect you to use it wisely."

They simmered down, and she padded over to the bulletin boards, curious as to what had elicited such a strong reaction from that pear-shaped old combover. The Panther City Hebrew Congregation? No, Stacy Z had placed that higher up, between two pet shops.

She wondered if a big belly would rearrange her center of gravity when she squatted like this. Maybe she'd find out this summer.

And then she saw. A Panther City vice district had sprung up sometime in the last week. A cigar store, a liquor store, and a strip club clearly inspired by that sleazy joint down on Meridian and 23rd.

She should have been paying better attention.

"Boys and girls, I want you all to close your eyes and count to 100!" she announced.

"Why?" they asked, their curiosity piqued by the urgency of her tone.

"Because your teacher says so!" she thundered.

Cowed, they did as told. "1, 2, 3…"

Probably there were some peekers, but she couldn't be bothered to police that right now. Clawing the offending structures from the board took precedence. She had them scrunched up in her fist before they reached 50. Locked in the drawer where she kept her grading book by 99.

In the principal's office while the children were at lunch, she argued that it must have been an eye of the beholder situation, that while she wouldn't want to speculate about what could cause a visiting principal's eyes to play tricks on him, she doubted many men would mistake a Tutu Shoppe for a go-go bar or the apothecary jars of an "Old Timey Candy Shoppe" as containing liquor, not candy.

Yes, one child had made a cigar store, but that was driven by an interest in Indians, not cigars. She'd taken it down, and would be monitoring carefully to make sure nothing of an adult nature slipped past her in future.

The principal narrowed her eyes, worming her lips around as if her power to fire a lying second year teacher was a caramel cream she was savoring.

In the end, the sentence she pronounced was surprisingly light. Mrs. Voss was given 'til the end of the week to redo the bulletin boards. Give the children a day or two to write a final reflection on the project, then move on. Maybe to something with a 500 Mile Race theme.

The principal had pegged Steven Smiley as the source of class 3B's immorality, but decided to let it go, seeing as how the evidence had been removed from view before she could clap eyes on it, and certain sleeping dogs were best left to lie.

Mrs. Voss felt guilty for not defending him, but she too, had a vested interest in letting sleeping dogs lie.

Steven, meanwhile, would have loved to be credited as the mastermind of Panther City's vice strip, and would gladly have accepted punishment as the cost of doing business.

But visually speaking, there was no chance he was the perp. He was a lamppost man. His meager contributions to Panther City lacked a discernible style.

Not like Annie's. Not like Jasper's or Lee Lindstrom's.

R ichard came home from work with a rough sketch of Shannon's Roaring 20s that he had drawn in solidarity. "I was all set to do the 21st Amendment, too, but I got hung up in a meeting, so I'm afraid the strip club's all you're getting."

"No cigar store?" she asked gamely. He laughed, and she thanked him for the gift. "It's really good. Maybe I should hang it up on the bulletin board."

"Sure, if you're bucking to get yourself fired."

She raised her eyebrows. "Maybe I am."

"Are you flirting with me?"

"Maybe." She cocked her hip at him saucily. He gave a wolf whistle, but that was it. He was a bit squeamish about having sex with his pregnant wife, as if the baby would spy on their intimacies through its mother's bellybutton.

She dropped her seductive pose, and studied his rendering. It really was good. He'd nailed all the identifying details.

So had Jasper, for that matter. Poor kid must've been driven past the joint a hundred times, en route to see his sister in the hospital.

"Hey, Rich," she said. "You've never been inside that place, have you?"

"Me?" His eyes widened innocently. "No! It's on the way to work, that's all."

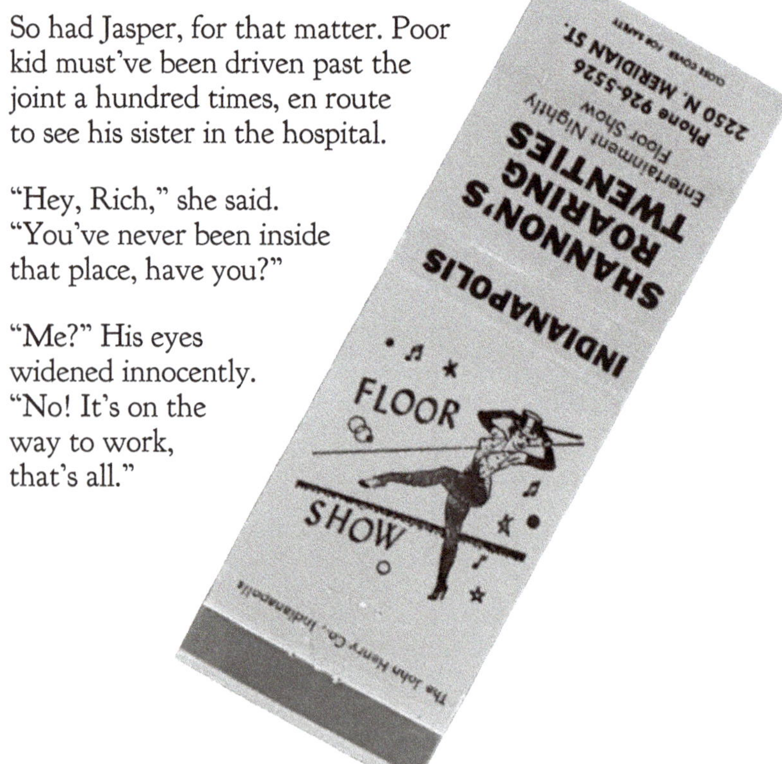

The wave of nausea brought on by the smell of Richard's breakfast was so seismic, she called in sick, only to feel fine minutes later.

It was psychological, probably. Who wouldn't prefer to throw up at home when the alternative was a single seater toilet sprinkled with boy pee, and a couple of girls eavesdropping on the other side of the door?

Surely she'd earned the right to play a little hooky. Especially now that she'd learned to appreciate it. In her pre-pregnant days, she'd have started climbing the walls, idling on the couch with a ginger ale and a box of Saltines as <u>The Today Show</u> gave way to Bob Braun, then the local news.

Now, she had no problem with just lolling around. This homey monotony beat Sarasota any day.

Was this how life would feel after the baby? So placid and unambitious?

She pictured herself wheeling a stroller to Kinkaid's for a pound of ground beef. Smiling as she positioned silverware on a table set with candles. Gazing into the nursery, Richard's arm around her waist, a golden door-shaped glow illuminating the crib. Motherhood unfolded before her in a series of irresistible Kodak moments.

Not once did she fret about how her sub was making out.

In the history of accidents, hers was surely the stupidest. She'd been watching <u>The Price Is Right</u> with her feet tucked up under her. When the phone rang, she bounced up to get it, even though it meant missing what was behind Curtain Number Two.

Unfortunately, both feet had fallen asleep, and she went down like a tree, tumbling over the coffee table, both arms flung out in an unconscious attempt to break her fall.

The pain was so bad she nearly blacked out. She'd had to scream for help out the open window. Thank god Mr. Morrison had been futzing out in his side yard, hearing aids in. He'd located the extra key they kept under their cement frog sculpture, gingerly loading her into his aged Pontiac for the ride to Methodist. After the receptionist at Richard's firm told him Richard was in an important meeting, he borrowed a second dime to call Myrna.

The baby was unharmed, but she'd broken the scaphoid bones in both wrists, in addition to suffering a Colles' fracture of the right radius.

Her forearms looked like swan's necks.

The doctor said the casts would have to stay on for six weeks. "You should arrange with your mother-in-law to handle all your cooking and cleaning," he advised.

She asked about pain medicine, but he was reluctant to give her much more than Tylenol, and even that should be used sparingly, given her delicate condition.

So that was that.

The decision had been taken out of her hands. Literally. She would have to quit teaching a bit sooner than anticipated, but no one could accuse her of throwing in the towel. It had been an accident. The children would understand. She wasn't abandoning them. As soon as she was able, she would have Myrna drive her over to school, to tell them goodbye in person. With over a month left in the school year, there was no great rush.

Richard arrived home early and made an endearing fuss, plunking a bouquet of peonies on the mantle, and dumping an armload of magazines into her lap, even though she had no way to page through them. He gave the casserole his mother had thrown together a thumbs down, and dialed up a pizza from Ring Brings, which he fed to her by hand, claiming it was good practice for the baby.

He told her they could figure out the bathroom stuff later. More practice for the baby.

She moved to cover her face with her hands, but it hurt to raise her arms.

"Don't be embarrassed," he said, "It'll be romantic."
He kissed her belly through the shapeless snap front dress Myrna had put her in. "Tell Mommy to call her principal before it gets too late," he whispered.

"Five more minutes" she begged. He shook his head, smiled, and joined her on the couch, where they sat in companionable silence, watching the sun set on Panther City.

ACKNOWLEDGMENTS

THANKS TO:

Ariel Gore, the Spring 2024 Wayward Writers Catskills Camp, the Fall 2024 Wayward Writers Truth or Consequences Camp, and the 2025 Chapbook Challenge, especially Mandy Trichell and Edward Thomas-Herrera.

All the Panther Citizens who came together on Kickstarter.

Big Sarah Cooke, who inadvertently planted a seed, and Spencer Kayden who tweezed the final weeds.

Architect Guy Copper for Rich's rendering of the infamous Indianapolis strip club, Shannon's Roaring 20s.

Dawn Yow, my young illustrator's extremely patient and helpful assistant/mother.

The Silverback, Greg Kotis.

The former 3rd graders who consented to having their school pictures reproduced herein, especially my classmates, and our wonderful teacher, who inscribed a book of haiku for me at year's end:

To Anne Halliday,
    Whose creative writing and artwork
have been an inspiration to all her classmates.
And who has utilized her time very wisely
in independent reading during the year 1973–1974.

(I cried.)